Some Dog!

Story by Errol Broome

Illustrations by Craig Smith

D0064322

Remembering Bondi, a great dog.

PM Chapter Books
part of the Rigby PM Collection

U.S. edition © 2001 Rigby
a division of Reed Elsevier Inc.
500 Coventry Lane
Crystal Lake, IL 60014
www.rigby.com

Text © 2001 Nelson Thomson Learning
Illustrations © 2001 Nelson Thomson Learning
Originally published in Australia by Nelson Thomson Learning

06 05 04 03 02 01
10 9 8 7 6 5 4 3 2 1

Some Dog!
ISBN 0 7635 7788 X

Printed in China by Midas Printing (Asia) Ltd

Contents

Chapter 1   Pete's Arrival   4

Chapter 2   Six Months Ago   6

Chapter 3   Jimpy's Arrival   10

Chapter 4   The Shoe Dog   17

Chapter 5   A Strange Sound   20

Chapter 6   Call the Police!   23

Chapter 7   Jimpy the Hero   26

Chapter 1
Pete's Arrival

"Have you got any pets?" asked Pete.

For a moment, Josh didn't answer. He glanced around the kitchen, quickly, then looked away. "No, no pets."

"Not even a dog? I thought I saw a collar."

Josh shook his head.

"Tell him about Jimpy," said Emmie.

Josh frowned at his sister and felt his cheeks redden with anger and hurt. She knew he didn't want to talk about it.

"Go on, Josh," Emmie insisted.

"Who's Jimpy?" asked Pete.

Josh turned away. Why had Mom asked this cousin from the country to stay? He and Emmie barely knew Pete, and here he was asking all these questions. Josh didn't want to tell him about Jimpy. He was trying to forget. It hurt too much to remember, and to see the places where Jimpy used to sit. All empty now.

Chapter 2

Six Months Ago

Josh hadn't mentioned the dog's name since... It must be six months ago now. Mom had put away Jimpy's food dish and drinking bowl. They'd thrown out his worn rug, but somehow they couldn't part with his collar. Mom hung it on a hook outside the back door. "We might get another dog one day," she'd said. But Josh knew she just couldn't bring herself to throw it out. None of them could.

How could any other dog replace Jimpy? Josh didn't know how his mother could even think of it. He'd never have another dog. You didn't go out and buy another, just like that, as if your previous dog had never existed.

Nothing seemed fun anymore. Mom kept telling Josh to stop moping around, that it was time he pulled himself together. It was all right for her to talk like that, but it only made him feel worse. She didn't understand how much he missed Jimpy.

Each time he walked up the back steps, he tried not to look at Jimpy's old collar. It was a reminder that Jimpy wasn't there. If he couldn't see the empty collar, then maybe...maybe he could pretend Jimpy wasn't really gone.

Chapter 3
Jimpy's Arrival

Josh jerked back to face his cousin. Pete was watching him, waiting for his reply. Josh opened his mouth, but no words came.

"Oh, all right," said Emmie. She flopped on a kitchen stool, and tucked her toes under the bars. "I'll tell him."

The day Jimpy arrived, he chewed on Mom's best shoes. He was only a few weeks old, and that first night away from his mother he cried without stopping. Josh and I took turns to comfort him. Every time we went back to bed, he cried again. In the end, I gave him one of my slippers. After that, he ate a shoe nearly every day.

"Is that why you have bare feet?" asked Pete.

Emmie wiggled her toes on the bar. "We were a bit short of shoes for a while."

Pete screwed up his nose. "Didn't he eat anything else?"

Sometimes a sock would do. He had all the right puppy food, too, but he expected a shoe to chew each day. Mom got pretty mad at him, especially when he learned how to open her closet.

Josh sat, as if he were not listening, or couldn't hear. Pete's eyes opened wider and wider as Emmie went on with the story. "Where...what did you do with the chewed-up shoes?" Pete wondered.

Jimpy buried them. At first, we couldn't find them. Then we saw this mound rising in the yard. It grew bigger and bigger, until it began to look like a grave.

Emmie glanced quickly at Josh. She hadn't meant to mention that word.

"A grave of old shoes!" said Pete.

"Yes." Emmie giggled.

He buried them like wild dogs bury bones, in case the supply ran out one day.

Mom didn't like old shoes in the yard, so she dug them up and put them in the garbage can. Jimpy was getting short of shoes, and so were we.

"How could you keep a dog like that?"

We loved him. He was all round and soft like brown velvet. His ears flopped when he walked, and his tail nearly wagged off. And he was so funny! Besides, after a while people began to hear about the shoe dog. They would bring old shoes and leave them at the door. Soon, there were rows of shoes on the front porch.

Jimpy was grown-up by now, and only needed a shoe every few days. So the rows of shoes stretched further, till they covered the whole porch.

Chapter 4
The Shoe Dog

Othe night, three tough kids knocked on the door. When Mom opened it, this punk girl said, "Where's the party?"

"What party?" asked Mom. "There's no party."

The girl pointed to the lines of shoes. "Then who owns all these?"

Mom laughed. "Our dog. Those shoes belong to our dog."

The three stared at her, and then at one another. "Is his name Centipede?" asked one of the boys.

Mom just stood there, blocking the doorway, until they gave up and went away.

After that, Mom decided we should move the shoes off the porch. She didn't want strangers thinking we were running a restaurant. We carried the shoes inside and piled them into a small storeroom off the kitchen.

"So that was the end of that," said Pete.

"Oh, no!" Josh interrupted. "You should hear what happened next!"

Chapter 5

A Strange Sound

Emmie and Pete stared at Josh, for it was the first time that he had even shown he was listening.

"Go on, Josh," said Emmie gently. "You tell."

Josh leaned his elbows on the table, and his eyes shone as memories flashed back.

Every time we opened the storeroom door, a shoe fell out. Jimpy tapped on the door when he wanted one. Emmie said it was like a slot machine—pull the handle and out comes a shoe.

Mom was pretty happy because the house was tidy again, and no strangers came to the door. Until...

One afternoon, Emmie and I came home from school and let ourselves in the front door. Jimpy ran up the hallway to the kitchen. He rushed to the storeroom and sat there, barking.

"Ssh, Jimpy," I said.

He kept on barking. When Emmie went to open the door, he leaped in the air and carried on like a circus dog.

"What's wrong with him?" I asked.

Emmie's cheeks were pale, so you could see her freckles. "He's telling us something," she said.

Just then, we heard the front door open, and Mom walked into the house. "Whatever's going on?"

"Jimpy's gone mad," I said.

Mom stood staring at the door as though she had x-ray eyes.

Then we heard a cough.

Chapter 6
Call the Police!

I looked at Emmie, then at Mom, and I could tell it wasn't them. Something clicked in my head, and suddenly, I knew.

"There's someone in the storeroom!" I whispered.

"He must have heard us come home!" croaked Emmie. "And now he's hiding!"

"I'll call the police!" cried Mom in a loud whisper.

Jimpy sat there like a guard dog and went on barking. No burglar would come out to face a noise like that!

When two police officers arrived, Jimpy barked at them, too.

"Call your dog off, will you?" said one. They told us to go to another room and take Jimpy with us. It was like being in a movie, only this was real. And it was in our house.

We huddled near the door and listened. One officer called, "Come out, now. No funny stuff!" But he was talking to the person in the storeroom, not to us.

There was a scuffle, then a tumbling sound as all the shoes poured onto the floor. A few seconds later, they led the man to the police car. Then an officer came back and said he needed another look inside. The man was wearing only socks, and must have left his shoes behind.

Mom told him to take his pick. There were plenty to choose from.

Chapter 7
Jimpy the Hero

The police officer stared at the mountain of shoes that had spilled all over the room.

Jimpy slunk over and sniffed at the pile. He picked up a boot with his teeth and tossed it across the room. Then he found another one. Jimpy knew a bad man's shoes when he sniffed them! And he didn't want those boots in the house.

The officer picked them up, and peered down at Jimpy. "This isn't the shoe dog, is it?"

He'd heard of Jimpy! He gave him a big pat, and said he was as good as any dog in the police force.

Pete grinned at Josh. "You had a kind of hero in the family."

"Sure did," said Josh, proudly.

"Then what...where is he now?"

Emmie opened her mouth to say something, but Josh interrupted. "It's all right, Emmie, I'll tell him."

"Did he get old or something?" asked Pete.

Josh shook his head. "Not really that old, just sick. It started slowly, so that at first we hardly noticed, but soon he couldn't walk, and the vet told us he wouldn't get better. We...we took him back to the vet...and Mom waited with him. It seemed like ages before she came out...with just his collar in her hands."

"But we have a whole lot of memories," said Emmie.

"Yes. Remember how he made us laugh! And sometimes he made Mom angry, but he was always good to be with, especially when everyone else was out. And when I was feeling bad about things, he made me feel better. And when he..." The words just kept coming.

Once Josh started, he couldn't stop talking about Jimpy. All the good times came tumbling back, and he knew the memories would always be with him.

Emmie grinned at him.

"Some dog!" said Pete. "I saw his collar near the back door."

"Yes," said Josh. He stood up and had his first good look at the cousin who had come to stay. Pete had a smile that took up most of his face, and a row of top teeth like a picket fence.

Just today, just now, since Pete arrived, Josh had begun to feel happy inside himself again. He wasn't sure how it had happened. He knew he would never see Jimpy again. But he could talk about him, and feel good about it.

"I'm glad you came," he said to Pete. "Do you have any pets at home?"

"Yes," said Pete. "A collie called Rusty. You should see him rounding up the sheep on our farm. He's great, but he's never done anything like your shoe dog."

Josh shrugged. "I guess all pets are different." He reached across and grabbed Emmie's arm. "Let's tell Mom that maybe it's time we thought about getting another dog."